SOPRANO

MUSICAL THEATRE ESS

VOLUME 2

Compiled and Edited by
Richard Walters

Published by
Hal Leonard Europe
A Music Sales / Hal Leonard Joint Venture Company
14-15 Berners Street, London W1T 3LJ, UK.

Exclusive Distributors:
Music Sales Limited
Distribution Centre, Newmarket Road
Bury St Edmunds, Suffolk IP33 3YB, UK.

Order No. HLE90004211
ISBN 978-1-61780-441-0
This book © Copyright 2012 Hal Leonard Europe

Your Guarantee of Quality
As publishers, we strive to produce every book to the highest commercial standards.
The book has been carefully designed to minimise awkward page turns and to make playing from it a real pleasure.
Throughout, the printing and binding have been planned to ensure a sturdy, attractive publication which should give years of enjoyment.
If your copy fails to meet our high standards, please inform us and we will gladly replace it.

www.musicsales.com

This publication is not authorised for sale in the
United States of America and/or Canada.

HAL LEONARD EUROPE
DISTRIBUTED BY MUSIC SALES

CONTENTS

ABOUT THE SHOWS AND SONGS

CAROUSEL
Mister Snow

Music by Richard Rodgers
Lyrics and Book by Oscar Hammerstein II
Opened in New York 19 April 1945
Opened in London 7 June 1950

The collaborators of *Oklahoma!* chose Ferenc Molnar's play *Liliom* as the basis for their second show together. Oscar Hammerstein shifted Molnar's Budapest locale to a late 19th century fishing village in New England. The two principal roles are Billy Bigelow, a shiftless carnival barker, and Julie Jordan, an ordinary mill worker. This is not merely a simple boy meets girl plot, but contains a predominant theme of tragedy throughout most of the play. Rodgers always cited *Carousel* as the score he was most proud of in his long career. Julie and Carrie Pipperidge, a friend and fellow mill worker, stroll by the sea shore near a carnival, where Julie has exchanged some familiarity with the carousel barker, Billy, whom she does not know. Carrie confesses her own romance in **"Mister Snow."** She and Snow do marry, after a few bumps in the romance. Billy marries Julie, and then dies in a robbery. Julie has a daughter, and years later at the girl's high school graduation, Billy's spirit appears and comforts both mother and daughter. A film version was released in 1956. Nicholas Hytner directed an acclaimed 1992 production at Royal National Theatre in London. This was adapted for Broadway in 1994. Another revival of *Carousel* opened in the West End in 2008.

CINDERELLA
In My Own Little Corner
Ten Minutes Ago

Music by Richard Rodgers
Lyrics and Book by Oscar Hammerstein II
First aired live on 31 March 1957 on CBS Television (US)

Ever the innovators, Rodgers and Hammerstein were among the first to explore the new medium of television with a full-length original TV musical. The show also was fortunate in securing the services of Julie Andrews, fresh from her triumph as the Cinderella-like heroine in *My Fair Lady*. In adapting the children's fairy tale, Hammerstein was careful not to alter or update the familiar story about a young woman whose Fairy Godmother helps her to overcome the plots of her evil stepmother and stepsisters so that she can go to an opulent ball and meet a handsome prince. Cinderella still loses her magical glass slipper, and the Prince still proclaims that he will marry the girl whose foot fits the slipper. Abused and unappreciated by her stepmother and stepsisters, Cinderella sits by the fireplace alone and sings **"In My Own Little Corner."** The fairy godmother has magically appeared and enabled Cinderella to attend the royal ball. The Prince is captivated by her. In love at first sight, Cinderella and the Prince sing **"Ten Minutes Ago"** following their first dance. The 1957 live broadcast drew the largest American television audience to date. A 1965 American television production was made in color, starring Lesley Ann Warren as Cinderella. A new production was filmed in 1997 for the American television network ABC, starring pop star Brandy as Cinderella, Whitney Houston as the fairy godmother, Bernadette Peters as the stepmother, and others. In 2004, a black-and-white kinescope taping of the rehearsal for the original 1957 production starring Julie Andrews was discovered and subsequently released on DVD. A stage adaptation toured the U.S.; the musical finally made its New York stage debut in 1993 at New York City Opera.

GUYS AND DOLLS
If I Were A Bell

Music and Lyrics by Frank Loesser
Book by Abe Burrows and Jo Swerling
Opened in New York 24 November 1950
Opened in London 28 May 1953

Populated by the hard-shelled but soft-centered characters who inhabit the world of writer Damon Runyon, this "Musical Fable of Broadway" tells the tale of how Miss Sarah Brown of the Save-a-Soul Mission saves the souls of assorted Times Square riff-raff while losing her heart to the smooth-talking gambler, Sky Masterson. **"If I Were A Bell"** shows Sarah under the unfamiliar and, for the moment, giddy effects of alcohol supplied by Sky. *Guys And Dolls* is considered one of the best musical comedies of the 20th century. For many years Laurence Olivier wanted to play the character Nathan Detroit, but that production was never mounted. An all black cast played in a Broadway revival of 1976. A major revival opened in London in 1982 at the National Theatre. A 1992 Broadway revival was an enormous success. Further revivals played in the West End in 1996 and 2005. The 1955 film version starred Frank Sinatra as Nathan Detroit, Marlon Brando as Sky Masterson, Jean Simmons as Sarah, and Vivian Blaine (the only remnant of the Broadway cast) as Adelaide.

INTO THE WOODS
On The Steps Of The Palace
Children Will Listen

Music and Lyrics by Stephen Sondheim
Book by James Lapine
Opened in New York 5 November 1987
Opened in London 25 September 1990

Into The Woods brought together for the second time the Pulitzer Prize winning team of Lapine and Sondheim, turning this time to children's fairy tales as a subject. The book of *Into The Woods* often focuses on the darker, grotesque aspects of these stories, but by highlighting them, it touches on the themes of interpersonal relationships, death, and what we pass on to our children. Act I begins with the familiar "once upon a time" stories, and masterfully interweaves the plots of Snow White, Little Red Riding Hood, Cinderella, Jack and the Beanstalk, Rapunzel, a Baker and his Wife and others. Act II concerns what happens after "happily ever after," as reality sets in, and the fairy tale plots dissolve into more human stories. Cinderella evaded the prince earlier in the show. She sings **"On The Steps Of The Palace"** after their second meeting where she narrowly avoided capture. At the end of the show, the Baker quietly tells his infant son the story of the boy's birth and the morals learned. The Witch sings **"Children Will Listen"** (later joined by the whole ensemble). Though the role of the Witch is principally for a belter, **"Children Will Listen"** is in a more soprano range, and certainly can be successfully sung by a soprano voice. Revivals played in London in 1998, 2007, and in 2010 at the Regent's Park Open Air Theatre.

THE KING AND I
I Whistle A Happy Tune
My Lord And Master
Getting To Know You
We Kiss In A Shadow
Something Wonderful
I Have Dreamed

Music by Richard Rodgers
Lyrics and Book by Oscar Hammerstein II
Opened in New York 29 March 1951
Opened in London 8 October 1953

The musical is adapted from Margaret Landon's semi-fictionalized biographical 1944 novel *Anna And The King Of Siam*, which was based on memoirs of Anna Leonowens (1831–1915). The story is set in Bangkok, Siam, in the early 1860s, in and around the king's palace. Anna Leonowens, a widowed Englishwoman, arrives with her young son to begin the post of schoolteacher to the Siamese royal children. As Anna and her son Louis approach their new home, Louis confesses his anxiety at living in a new and unfamiliar environment. Anna reassures her son and herself by singing **"I Whistle A Happy Tune."** She has frequent clashes with the monarch but eventually comes to exert great influence on him, particularly in creating a more democratic society for his people. Tuptim, a young Burmese woman presented to the King of Siam as the latest addition to his collection of wives (a gift from the Prince of Burma) arrives escorted by courtier Lun Tha. Tuptim and Lun Tha have fallen in love. The King receives his new wife with little ceremony, and leaves her alone to regard her dire circumstances in **"My Lord And Master."** Anna, beginning to settle into her new life in Siam, connects with the king's children singing **"Getting To Know You."** Lun Tha and Tuptim have been meeting in secret with Anna as lookout. The threat of the King's wrath prompts them to sing **"We Kiss In A Shadow."** Lady Thiang, the King's chief wife (of many), knows him best. She affectionately relates all his flaws and redeeming qualities to Anna in **"Something Wonderful."** In Act II the lovers Lun Tha and Tuptim have decided to escape the court of Siam, risking great danger, and sing **"I Have Dreamed"** in anticipation of being away together. Both duets (**"We Kiss In A Shadow," "I Have Dreamed"**) have been adapted as solos for this edition. The 1953 London production starred Valerie Hobson. A revival played in the West End in 1973. Yul Brynner, the original King of Siam, played 4,633 performances in total over decades. A Broadway revival, reconceiving the show in a post-Yul Brynner era, opened in 1996. A London production, based on the Broadway revival, opened in 2000. A film version, arguably the best of any of the Rodgers and Hammerstein musicals, was released in 1956, starring Yul Brynner and Deborah Kerr.

THE LIGHT IN THE PIAZZA
The Beauty Is

Music and Lyrics by Adam Guettel
Book by Craig Lucas, based on the novella of the same name by Elizabeth Spencer
Opened in New York 18 April 2005
Opened in Leicester May 2009

Finding inspiration in the same country as his grandfather Richard Rodgers' *Do I Hear A Waltz?*, Adam Guettel's *The Light In The Piazza* follows Americans abroad in Italy. The story, after a novella by Elizabeth Spencer, concerns Margaret, a wealthy North Carolinian mother, and her beautiful, childlike 26 year old daughter Clara on extended vacation in Florence and Rome in the summer of 1953. Soon after their arrival in Florence, through a chance encounter, Clara meets Fabrizio, a 20 year old Italian man who speaks little English. Though there is a spark between them, Margaret protectively takes Clara away. As Clara strolls among the great art in the Uffizi Gallery, the paintings speak to her about herself, Italy, and her romantic yearnings as she sings **"The Beauty Is."** Fabrizio is determined, and with the help of his father, finally is able to spend time with Clara, though Margaret continues to attempt to discourage the romance. Margaret finally reveals the reason for her concern: due to being kicked in the head as a child by a pony, Clara has had arrested mental and emotional development. Margaret takes Clara to Rome to get her away from Fabrizio, but Clara's feelings for him remain fervent, and after much struggle she convinces her mother not to object to their marriage. A non-musical film adaptation of the novella was released in 1962.

MARY POPPINS
Anything Can Happen

Music and Lyrics by Richard M. Sherman and Robert B. Sherman,
   with new songs and additional music and lyrics by George Stiles and Anthony Drewe
Book by Julian Fellowes
Opened in London 18 September 2004
Opened in New York 16 November 2006

The magical and prickly character of the British nanny Mary Poppins was created by author P.L. Travers in eight books published from 1934 to 1988. Mary mysteriously arrives, blown by the wind, at 17 Cherry Tree Lane in London to care for the children of the Banks family. Though stern, Mary Poppins creates fantastical adventures and lessons for the children, often with the company of her chimney sweep friend Bert. Through Mary Poppins' influence, each member of the dysfunctional and disconnected Banks home gets set on the right path, though she leaves for a time to teach them a lesson. Julie Andrews starred in the 1964 Disney film musical, with songs by Richard and Robert Sherman. Nine songs from the movie were incorporated into the stage score, with the addition of seven new songs. Near the end of the show, after father George Banks has been suspended without pay from the bank of his employment for supposedly making the wrong choice about investments with a client, he learns that his choice actually has made the bank a fortune and all is well. Mary looks on with the children, teaching them that **"Anything Can Happen"** if you let it. With all happy and in order, Mary Poppins realizes that the Banks no longer need her, and she leaves them.

ME AND MY GIRL
Once You Lose Your Heart

Music by Noel Gay
Lyrics by Various
Book by L. Arthur Rose and Douglas Furber, revised by Stephen Fry
Opened in London 16 December 1937
Revised production opened in London 12 February 1985
Opened in New York 31 December 1989

The cockney character of Bill Snibson originated in 1935 in *Twenty To One*, played by comedian Lupino Lane. The actor became so attached to the role that he initiated a new musical show built around Bill two years later, resulting in *Me And My Girl*, a light social-class song and dance show in which Bill finds himself heir to an aristocratic title. Comedy results from the friction between the proletarian Bill and his posh new relations. Bill also has to decide whether to submit to an arranged match with a snobby blueblood, or stay true to his special gal from back in Lambeth. Revivals came to London in 1941, 1945 and 1949, but the major rediscovery of the show came in 1985 when Robert Lindsay reinvented the role in London, then in New York. Convinced that her Bill is gone forever, the homegirl sweetheart sighs the rueful little music-box ballad, **"Once You Lose Your Heart,"** sung by Emma Thompson as Sally in the 1985 London revival.

THE MOST HAPPY FELLA
Somebody, Somewhere

Music, Lyrics and Book by Frank Loesser
Opened in New York 3 May 1956
Opened in London 21 April 1960

Adapted from Sidney Howard's Pulitzer Prize winning play, *They Knew What They Wanted, The Most Happy Fella* was a particularly ambitious, near operatic work for the Broadway theatre, with more than thirty separate musical numbers including arias, duets, trios, quartets, choral pieces, and recitatives. Antonio Esposito, an aging Napa Valley vineyard owner, proposes to a lonely San Francisco waitress, Rosabella, by leaving a letter for her in the diner. (Her real name is Amy, but Tony calls her Rosabella, and that is the name of the role for almost the entire show.) Rosabella has no idea who wrote the letter, but is moved, singing **"Somebody, Somewhere."** She and Tony begin a correspondence of letters. Embarrassed of his physical appearance, Tony substitutes a photograph of a handsome friend, Joe. A Cyrano de Bergerac-like love triangle develops when Rosabella moves to Napa Valley to marry the man she thinks is Tony. More drama than comedy, Rosabella becomes pregnant by Joe, but in the end it is Tony she loves. He agrees to raise the child as his own with her.

THE MUSIC MAN
My White Knight

Music, Lyrics and Book by Meredith Willson
Opened in New York 19 December 1957
Opened in London 16 March 1961

With *The Music Man*, Meredith Willson recaptured the innocent charm of the Middle America he knew growing up in an Iowa town. It is around the Fourth of July (Independence Day), 1912, in River City, Iowa, and "Professor" Harold Hill, a traveling salesman of musical instruments, has arrived to con the citizens into believing that he can teach the town's children how to play in a marching band. But instead of skipping town before the instruments are to arrive, as is his usual routine, Hill remains because of the love of a good woman, librarian and piano teacher Marian Paroo. The story ends with the children, though barely able to produce any kind of a recognizable musical sound with Hill's "think system," being hailed by their proud parents. Marian's mother, who likes Hill, attempts to learn why her daughter is not interested in him. She replies with her description of her ideal man (Hill clearly falls short in her mind) in **"My White Knight."** (Parts of the song were retained, and others replaced in the new song "Being In Love," created for the film version of the musical.) By the end of the musical Harold and Marian can no longer deny their love for one another. Marian was originated on Broadway by Barbara Cook. Broadway revivals were performed in 1980 and 2000. A prominent regional production opened in 2008 in the UK at Chichester Festival Theatre. The film adaptation of the musical was released in 1962, retaining its original Broadway star Robert Preston as Hill.

MYTHS AND HYMNS
Migratory V

Music, Lyrics and Book by Adam Guettel
Opened in New York 31 March 1998
Opened in London 22 April 2007

The source material for Guettel's *Myths And Hymns* is just that—mythological figures such as Icarus, Pegasus and Sisyphus, and old texts from an 1886 Presbyterian Hymnal Guettel found in a used book store. The song cycle for the theatre premiered under the name *Saturn Returns* but was later changed to the present title. *Floyd Collins'* director Landau helped stage this night of music, which focused on the divine and profane in everyday life and uses musical language from straight-up pop to lush theatrical writing. **"Migratory V"** acknowledges our solitary achievements, but asks if we can come together in one voice, as does a flock of birds, can we not achieve a glimpse of the eternal?

NINE
Unusual Way (In A Very Unusual Way)

Music and Lyrics by Maury Yeston
Book by Arthur Kopit and Mario Fratti
Opened in New York 9 May 1982
Opened in London 7 June 1992

The influence of the director-choreographer was emphasized again with Tommy Tune's highly stylized, visually striking production of *Nine*, which, besides being a feast for the eyes is also one of the very few non-Sondheim Broadway scores to have true musical substance and merit from the 1970s and 1980s. The musical evolved from Yeston's fascination with Federico Fellini's semi-autobiographical 1963 film *8 1/2*. The story spotlights Guido Contini, a celebrated but tormented director who has come to a Venetian spa for a rest, and his relationships with his wife, his mistress, his protégée, his producer, and his mother. The production, which flashes back to Guido's youth and also takes place in his imagination, offers such inventive touches as an overture in which Guido conducts his women as if they were instruments, and an impressionistic version of the Folies Bergères. **"Unusual Way"** is sung to Guido by his young actress protégée. A huge production of *Nine* played in London at Royal Festival Hall in 1992, with 165 in the cast. This production was recorded. A small scale revival played in London in 1996. A Broadway revival opened in 2003 with Antonio Banderas as Guido. A film version of the musical was released in 2009.

OKLAHOMA!
People Will Say We're In Love
Many A New Day

Music by Richard Rodgers
Lyrics and Book by Oscar Hammerstein II
Opened in New York 31 March 1943
Opened in London 30 August 1947

Oklahoma!, based on the Lynn Riggs play *Green Grow the Lilacs*, is a recognized landmark in the history of American musical theatre. The initial Richard Rodgers and Oscar Hammerstein II collaboration, it not only expertly fused the major elements in the production—story, songs and dances—it also utilized dream ballets to reveal hidden desires and fears of the principals. *Oklahoma!* captured the Americana values of the U.S. during World War II, a distinct change from the urbane, edgy wit of the musicals of the 1930s. Set in Indian Territory soon after the turn of the century, *Oklahoma!* spins a simple tale mostly concerned with whether the decent cowboy Curly or the menacing farm hand Jed gets to take farm girl Laurey to the box social. Though she accepts Jud's invitation in a fit of pique, Laurey really loves Curly. When he finds out that Laurey is going to the social with Jud, Curly tries to convince her to change her mind. Not yet able to fully confess their feelings, they exchange a flirtatious warning in **"People Will Say We're In Love."** Each sings a verse; this solo version for soprano present Laurey's lyrics only. Laurey and her girlfriends are at her Aunt Eller's to rest and spruce up for the upcoming box social. She sees another girl making eyes with Curly, but flippantly declares to her friends in **"Many A New Day"** that she will wait for another man.

At the social Jud lashes out at Laurey when she doesn't return his feelings. She fires him; he threatens her. She turns to Curly for comfort and they finally admit their feelings for one another. At their wedding they join in celebrating Oklahoma's impending statehood, then—after Jud is accidentally killed in a fight with Curly—the couple rides off in their surrey with the fringe on top. With its Broadway run of five years, nine months, *Oklahoma!* established a long-run record that it held for 15 years, until being overtaken by *My Fair Lady*. *Oklahoma!* was among the first batch of new Broadway musicals to open in London after the end of World War II, achieving great success with Howard Keel as Curly. A prominent London production directed by Trevor Nunn opened in 1998 at the National Theatre, with Hugh Jackman as Curly. This production was adapted for a 2002 Broadway revival with a different cast. The film version was released in 1955.

SHE LOVES ME
I Don't Know His Name
Will He Like Me?
Dear Friend

Music by Jerry Bock
Lyrics by Sheldon Harnick
Book by Joe Masteroff
Opened in New York 23 April 1963
Opened in London 29 April 1964

The closely integrated, melody drenched score of *She Loves Me* is certainly one of the best ever written for a musical comedy. Set in the 1930s in Budapest, the tale is of the people who work in Maraczek's Parfumerie, principally the constantly squabbling sales clerk Amalia Balash and the manager Georg Nowack. It is soon revealed that they are anonymous romantic pen pals who agree to meet one night at the Café Imperiale, though neither knows the other's identity. Amalia explains how well she knows her penpal even though **"I Don't Know His Name."** Later, she worries about the upcoming first date in **"Will He Like Me?"** Georg sees that it is Amalia who is waiting for him in the restaurant, but doesn't let on. He attempts to engage her, but they argue and she sends him away, leaving her to sit there waiting in vain, culminating in **"Dear Friend."** Eventually, Georg is emboldened to reveal his identity by quoting from one of Amalia's letters and they fall in love. Amalia would have been played by Julie Andrews had she not been filming Mary Poppins. Amalia Balash in *She Loves Me* turned out to be one of Barbara Cook's most magical portrayals. Parfumerie, the Hungarian play by Miklos Laszlo on which *She Loves Me* is based, had been used as the basis for two films, *The Shop Around The Corner* (1940) and *In The Good Old Summertime* (1949). Yet another film, *You've Got Mail* (1998), was loosely adapted from the same story.

SHOW BOAT
Can't Help Lovin' Dat Man

Music by Jerome Kern
Lyrics and Book by Oscar Hammerstein II
Opened in New York 27 December 1927
Opened in London 3 May 1928

No show ever to hit Broadway was more historically important, and at the same time more beloved than *Show Boat*, that landmark of the 1927 season. (Any musical that ran more than one year, held over into the next season, was an enormous success in this period.) Edna Ferber's popular 1926 novel of life on the Mississippi River was the source for this musical/operetta, and provided a rich plot and characters which Kern and Hammerstein amplified to become some of the most memorable ever to grace the stage. Show Boat was a mixture of the American operetta style, based on British and Viennese models, and the new American musical theatre style, and presented a rare example of complete congruity which would later blossom in the more adventurous book musicals of the 1930s, '40s and '50s. Captain Andy Hawks heads a traveling troop of players on his show boat, the *Cotton Blossom*, which ambles up and down the river towns of the Mississippi. Soon after docking at Natchez, Mississippi, Andy's daughter Magnolia meets a riverboat gambler, Gaylord Ravenal. She excitedly tells her actress friend Julie about the dashing man she has just met. Julie cautions her that he may be a worthless drifter, and says it's not easy to stop loving a man, illustrated in **"Can't Help Lovin' Dat Man."** (In the context of the show this song is presented as an old favorite in an upbeat minstrel style, not in the slow and dreamy style of the 1951 film version. The 1936 film version of Show Boat is most close to the original Broadway production. The 1951 film version made significant changes to the musical.

THE SOUND OF MUSIC

I Have Confidence
Climb Ev'ry Mountain
Something Good

Music by Richard Rodgers
Lyrics by Oscar Hammerstein II
Book by Howard Lindsay and Russel Crouse
Opened in New York 16 November 1959
Opened in London 18 May 1961

Set in Austria in 1938 before and during the Anschluss (the Nazi annexing of Austria to Germany), *The Sound Of Music* is based on the book *The Trapp Family Singers* by Maria Augusta Trapp. Following her Mother Abbess's instructions to go into the world to confirm her convictions about intending to take vows to become a nun, Maria reluctantly agrees to leave the abbey to serve as governess to the widower Captain von Trapp's seven children. After bonding with the children and bringing music back into the previously glum household, Maria becomes afraid of the new feelings she has for the engaged-to-be-married Captain von Trapp. She returns to the abbey. The wise Mother Abbess offers Maria encouragement in deciding to face Captain von Trapp, singing **"Climb Ev'ry Mountain."** As millions who have seen the film know, she returns to marry the Captain, and the family escapes Salzburg as the Nazis take control. *The Sound Of Music* was the final Rodgers and Hammerstein collaboration. Hammerstein wrote both book and lyrics for all their musicals together except *The Sound Of Music*, for which he wrote lyrics only. He was ill during the writing and died of stomach cancer on 23 August 1960, months after the show's Broadway opening. Though a success on Broadway and London, the popularity of the musical skyrocketed following the release of the 1965 film version, for which Rodgers contributed two additional songs writing both lyrics and music: **"I Have Confidence,"** a whistle-in-the-dark song for Maria as she heads for her first day on the new job, and **"Something Good,"** an intimate love song for the Captain and Maria once they accept their feelings for one another. Both were added to the 1998 Broadway revival. The stage score, written for the modest range of Mary Martin, was transposed into a soprano range for Julie Andrews for the famous 1965 film version. Petula Clark played Maria in a 1981 London revival. A Broadway revival opened in 1998, and a London revival opened in 2006, with casting from the talent search UK television show "How Do You Solve A Problem Like Maria?"

WICKED

Let Us Be Glad
Popular

Music and Lyrics by Stephen Schwartz
Book by Winnie Holzman,
   based on the novel *Wicked: The Life And Times Of The Wicked Witch* Of The West by Gregory Maguire
Opened in New York 30 October 2003
Opened in London 27 September 2006

Stephen Schwartz's return to Broadway came with the hit musical *Wicked*. Based on Gregory Maguire's 1995 book, the musical chronicles the backstory of the Wicked Witch of the West, Elphaba, and Good Witch of the North, Glinda (Galinda), before their story threads are picked up in L. Frank Baum's *The Wonderful Wizard Of Oz*. As the musical begins, the citizens of Oz celebrate the death of the Wicked Witch of the West, led by Glinda singing **"Let Us Be Glad."** A flashback begins that tells the story of the complex relationship between the misunderstood Elphaba and the ambitious Galinda. Elphaba, shy and green, learns from radiant Galinda just what it takes to be **"Popular."** The two form a friendship in secret and unite against the duplicitous Wizard. Fiyero winds up with Elphaba, whose staged death of being melted is a hoax.

MISTER SNOW

from *Carousel*

Lyrics by OSCAR HAMMERSTEIN II
Music by RICHARD RODGERS

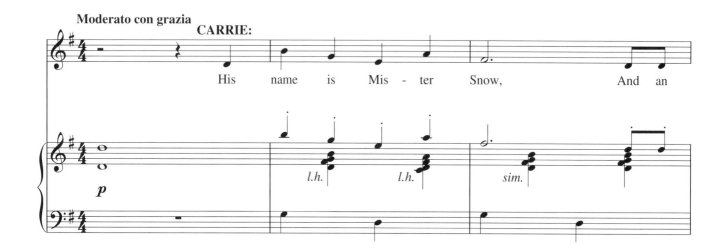

His name is Mis- ter Snow, And an

up- stand- in' man is he. He comes home ev- 'ry night in his

round- bot- tomed boat With a net full of her- ring from the sea.

An al-most per-fect beau, As re-fined as a girl could

wish, But he spends so much time in his round-bot-tomed boat, That he

can't seem to lose the smell of fish! The

fust time he kissed me, the whiff of his clo'es Knocked me flat on the floor of the

room, But now that I love him, my heart's in my nose, And fish is my fav-'rite per-

fume! Last night he spoke quite low, And a

fair spok-en man is he, And he said, "Miss Pipp-er-idge, I'd

like it fine If I could be wed with a wife, And, in-

deed, Miss Pipp - er - idge, if you'll be mine, I'll be yours fer the rest of my

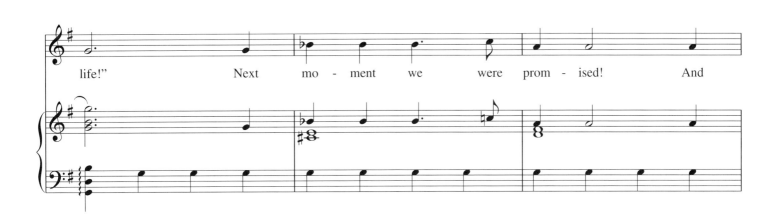

life!" Next mo - ment we were prom - ised! And

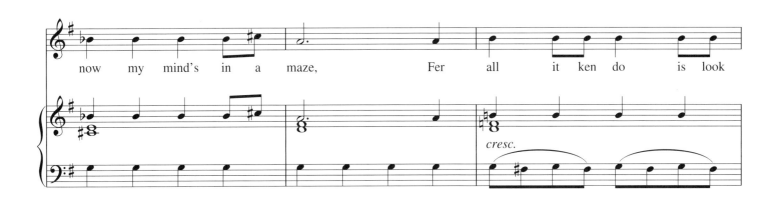

now my mind's in a maze, Fer all it ken do is look

for - ward to That won - der - ful day of days.

Refrain

Moderato *(with expression)*

When I mar - ry Mis - ter Snow,

p dolce

The flow - ers 'll be buz - zin' with the hum of bees, The

birds 'll make a rack - et in the church - yard trees, When I mar - ry Mis - ter

Snow.

Then it's off to home we'll

mf

p

lamb. Then he'll set me on my feet And I'll say, kind a sweet,

"Well, Mis - ter Snow, ___ here I am!" Then I'll

kiss him so he'll know That

ev - 'ry - thin' 'll be as right as right ken be, A - liv - in' in a cot - tage by the

* This spot is often effectively sung as a subito **p**.

IF I WERE A BELL

from *Guys And Dolls*

Words and Music by
FRANK LOESSER

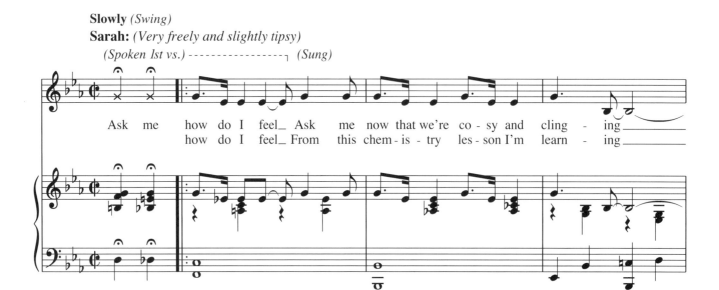

IN MY OWN LITTLE CORNER

from *Cinderella*

Lyrics by OSCAR HAMMERSTEIN II
Music by RICHARD RODGERS

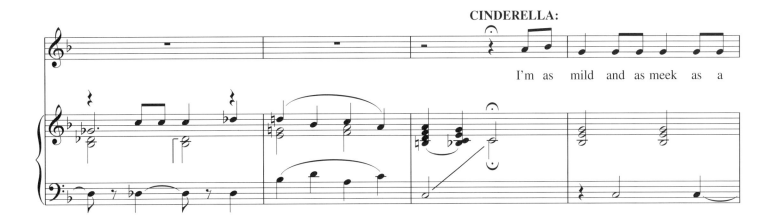

CINDERELLA:

I'm as mild and as meek as a

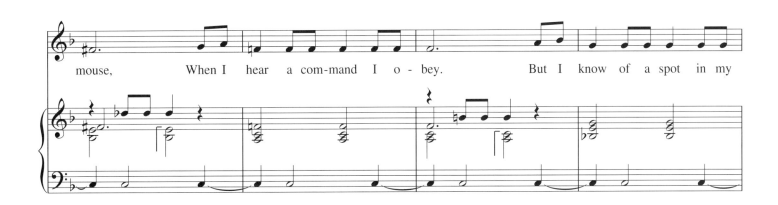

mouse, When I hear a com-mand I o-bey. But I know of a spot in my

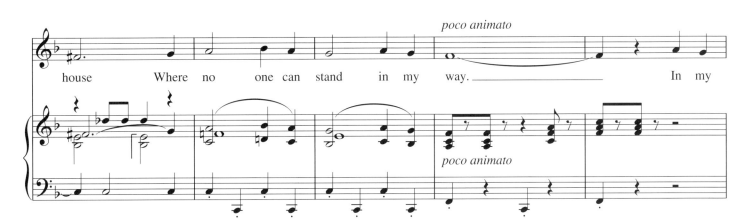

house Where no one can stand in my way. ____ In my

poco animato

own lit - tle cor - ner, in my own lit - tle chair, I can

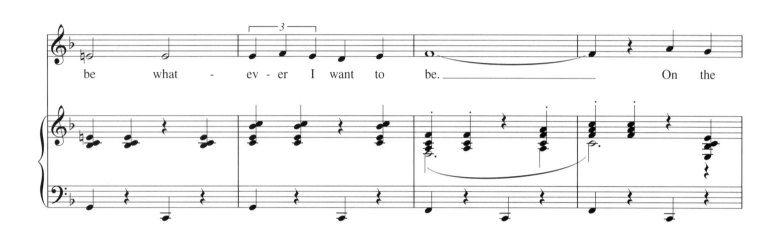

be what - ev - er I want to be. _____ On the

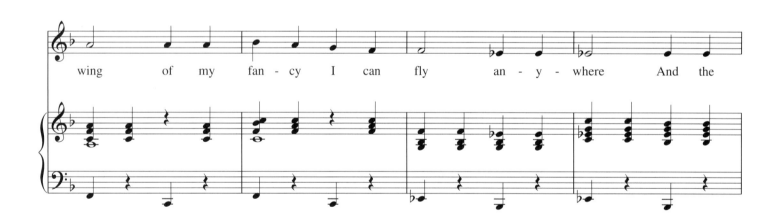

wing of my fan - cy I can fly an - y - where And the

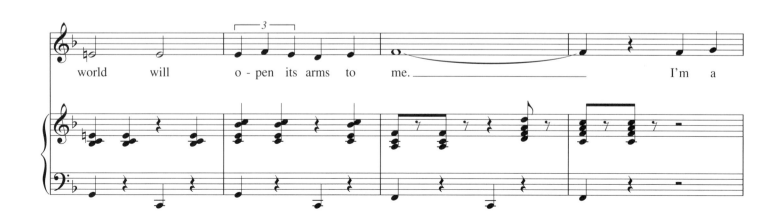

world will o - pen its arms to me. _____ I'm a

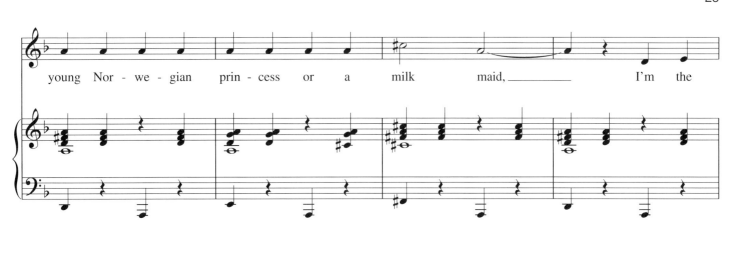

young Nor - we - gian prin - cess or a milk maid, _____ I'm the

great - est pri - ma don - na in Mi - lan, _____ I'm an

heir - ess who has al - ways had her silk made _____ By her

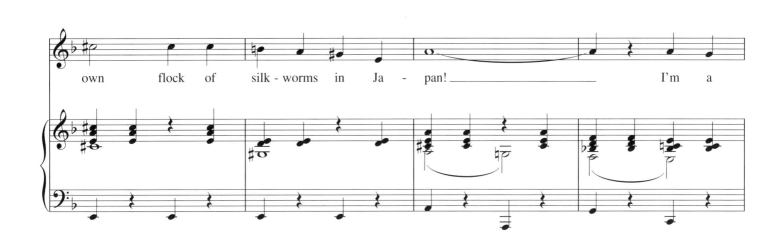

own flock of silk - worms in Ja - pan! _____ I'm a

girl men go mad for, Love's a game I can play With a

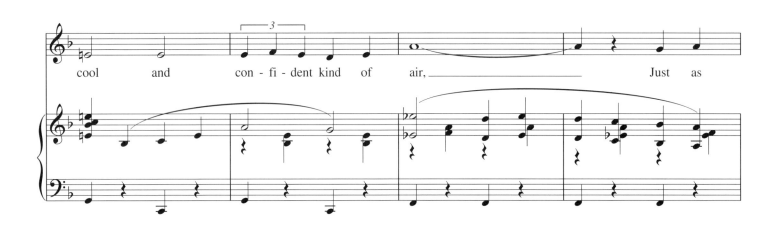

cool and con-fi-dent kind of air, _____ Just as

long as I stay in my own lit-tle cor - ner, _____ All a -

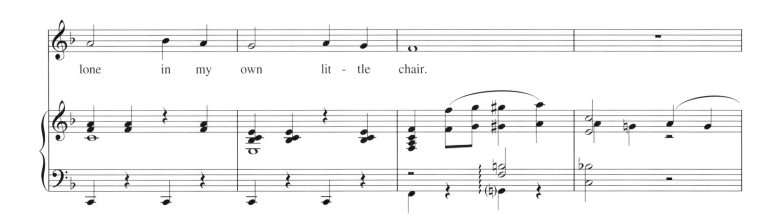

lone in my own lit-tle chair.

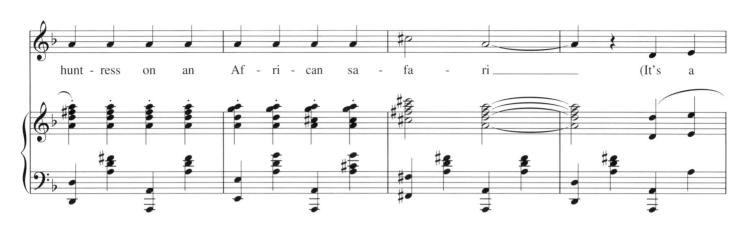

huntress on an Af-ri-can sa-fa-ri _____ (It's a

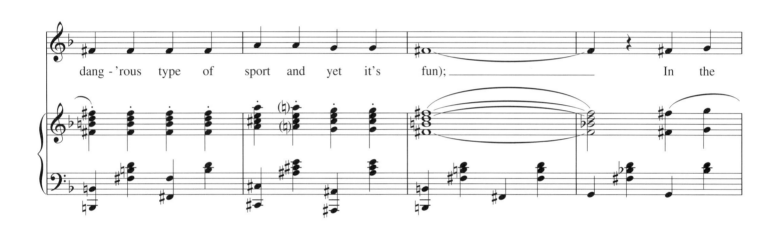

dang-'rous type of sport and yet it's fun); _____ In the

night I sal-ly forth to seek my quar-ry, _____ And I

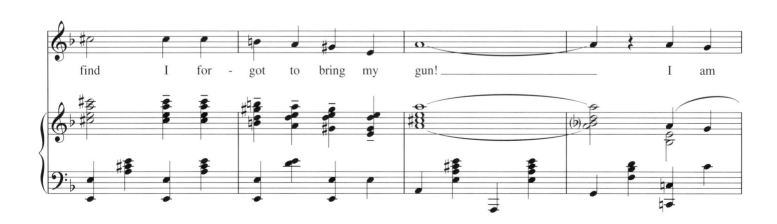

find I for-got to bring my gun! _____ I am

lost in the jun - gle All a - lone and un - armed When I

meet a li - on - ess in her lair! _____ Then I'm

(rit. al fine)

glad to be back in my own lit - tle cor - ner, _____ All a -

lone in my own lit - tle chair. _____

TEN MINUTES AGO
from *Cinderella*

Lyrics by OSCAR HAMMERSTEIN II
Music by RICHARD RODGERS

Moderato, in 1

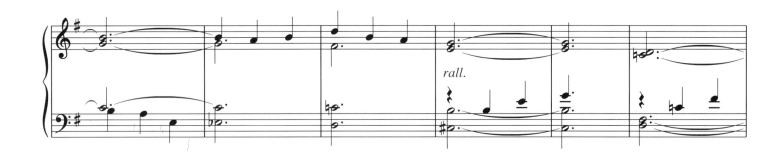

CINDERELLA: Waltz, in one

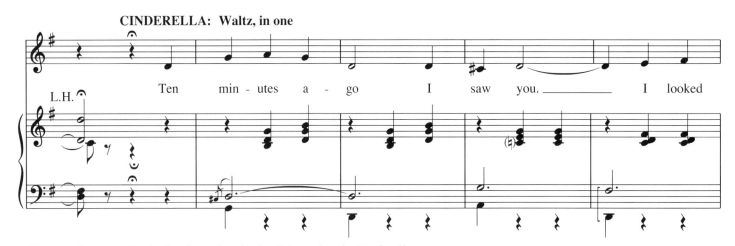

Ten min-utes a-go I saw you. ____ I looked

The song is sung twice in the show, first by the Prince, then by Cinderella.

up when you came through the door. _____ My head start-ed reel-ing, You

gave me the feel-ing the room had no ceil-ing or floor. _____ Ten

min-utes a - go I met you _____ And we mur-mured our how-do-you-

do's. _____ I want-ed to ring out the bells And

ON THE STEPS OF THE PALACE
from *Into The Woods*

Words and Music by
STEPHEN SONDHEIM

For ex-am-ple, a shoe. And then see what he'll do.

Now it's he and not you who is stuck with a shoe, In a stew, In the goo,

And you've learned some-thing, too, Some-thing you nev-er knew, _____

On the steps of the pal-ace. _____

CHILDREN WILL LISTEN

from *Into The Woods*

Words and Music by
STEPHEN SONDHEIM

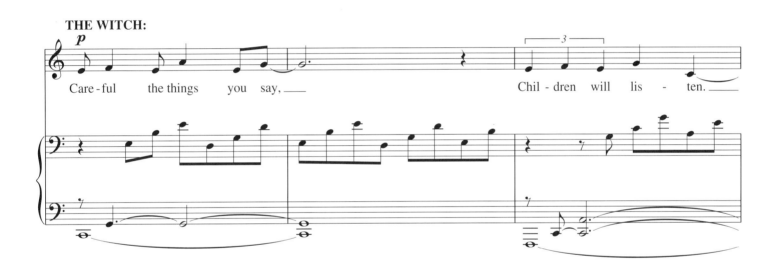

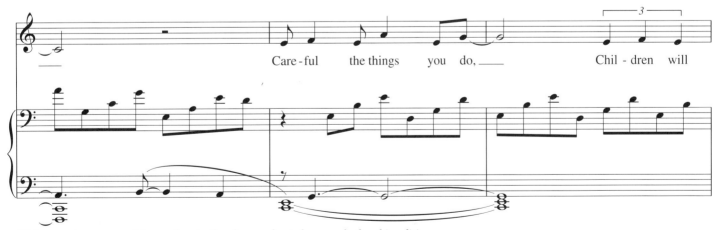

This song is an ensemble number in the show, adapted as a solo for this edition.

I WHISTLE A HAPPY TUNE

from *The King And I*

Lyrics by OSCAR HAMMERSTEIN II
Music by RICHARD RODGERS

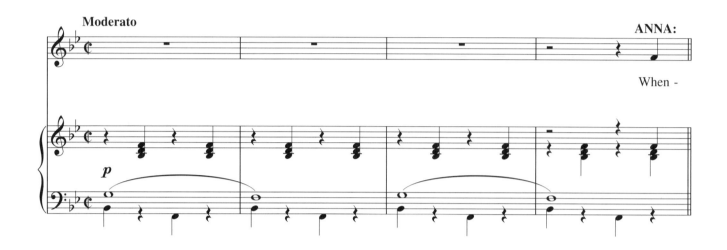

While shiv-er-ing in my shoes I strike a care-less pose And whis-tle a hap-py tune And no one ev - er knows I'm a-fraid _____ The re-sult of this de-cep - tion is ver - y strange to __ tell For when I fool the

peo - ple I fear I fool my - self as well! I whis - tle a hap - py

tune And ev - 'ry sin - gle time The hap - pi - ness in the

tune con - vin - ces me that I'm not a - fraid.

Make be - lieve you're brave And the trick will take you far.

You may be as brave as you make be - lieve you are.

Whistle

You may be as brave as you make be - lieve you

are.

MY LORD AND MASTER
from *The King And I*

Lyrics by OSCAR HAMMERSTEIN II
Music by RICHARD RODGERS

GETTING TO KNOW YOU
from *The King And I*

Lyrics by OSCAR HAMMERSTEIN II
Music by RICHARD RODGERS

ANNA: (rather spoken)
It's a ver - y an - cient say - ing, but a true and hon - est thought, That if you be - come a teach - er, By your pu - pils you'll be taught, (sung) As a teach - er I've been

learn - ing (You'll for - give me if I boast) And I've now be - come an

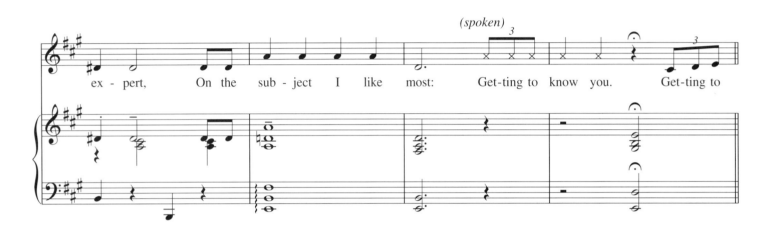

(spoken)

ex - pert, On the sub - ject I like most: Get-ting to know you. Get-ting to

Gracefully and not fast ♩ = 120

know you, get-ting to know all a - bout you. Get-ting to

like you, get-ting to hope you like me Get-ting to

know you, Put-ting it my way, but nice - ly,_____ You are pre-

cise - ly_____ My cup of tea!_____ Get-ting to

know you, get-ting to feel free and eas - y._____ When I am

with you, Get-ting to know what to say._____ Have-n't you

with you. Get-ting to know what to say _____ Have-n't you

no - ticed? Sud-den-ly I'm bright and breez - y _____ Be-cause of

all the beau-ti-ful and new things I'm learn-ing a-bout you

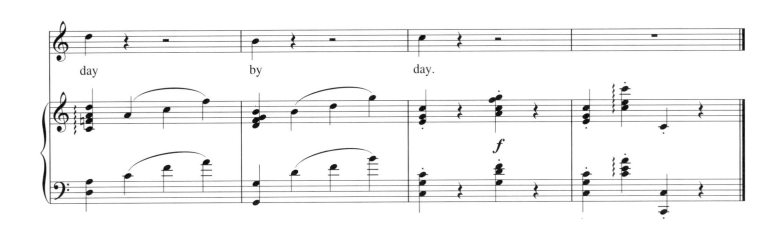

day by day.

WE KISS IN A SHADOW

from *The King And I*

Lyrics by OSCAR HAMMERSTEIN II
Music by RICHARD RODGERS

This song is a duet for Lun Tha and Tuptim, adapted as a solo for this edition.

When peo - ple are near, we speak not a word.

A - lone in our se - cret, To - geth - er we sigh For

one smil - ing day to be free, _____

To kiss in the sun - light And say to the sky: _____

Be - hold and be - lieve what you see! Be -

hold how my lov - er loves me!

[rit.] [a tempo]

A - lone in our se - cret, To - geth - er we sigh For

one smil - ing day to be free,

SOMETHING WONDERFUL
from *The King And I*

Lyrics by OSCAR HAMMERSTEIN II
Music by RICHARD RODGERS

He will not al - ways say What you would have him say, But, now and then, he'll say some-thing won - der-ful. The thought-less things he'll do Will hurt and wor - ry you. Then, all at once, he'll do some-thing won - der-ful. He has a thou-sand dreams that won't come true. You

I HAVE DREAMED

from *The King And I*

Lyrics by OSCAR HAMMERSTEIN II
Music by RICHARD RODGERS

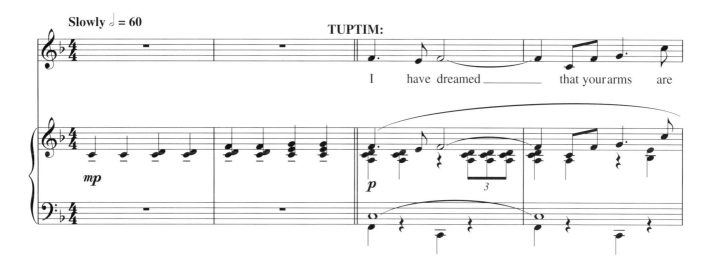

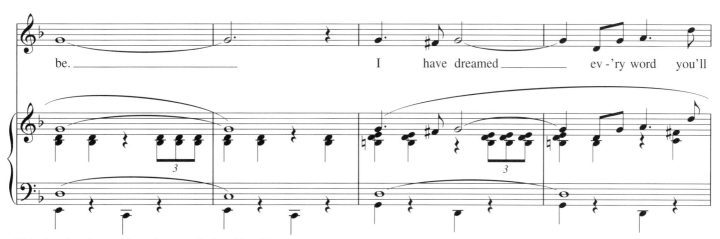

This duet has been adapted as a solo for this edition.

THE BEAUTY IS
from *The Light In The Piazza*

Words and Music by
ADAM GUETTEL

With a strong pulse

CLARA:

These are ver - y pop - u - lar   in It - a - ly!

old mu - se - um. Far a - way from home as some-one can go.

And the beau - ty is I still meet peo - ple I know. ___ Hel -

Expressively

lo. This is want-ing some-thing. This is reach-ing for it.

mp

This is wish-ing that a mo-ment would ar - rive. This is tak - ing chanc- es.

hard-ly met a sin-gle soul, but I am not a-lone._____ I feel

p

accel. poco a poco

Tempo II (Poco più mosso)

known! This is want-ing some-thing. This is pray-ing for it.

f

This is hold-ing breath and keep-ing fin-gers crossed. This is count-ing bless-ings.

This is won-d'ring when I'll see that__ boy a-gain.__

ANYTHING CAN HAPPEN

from *Mary Poppins*

Music by GEORGE STILES
Lyrics by ANTHONY DREW

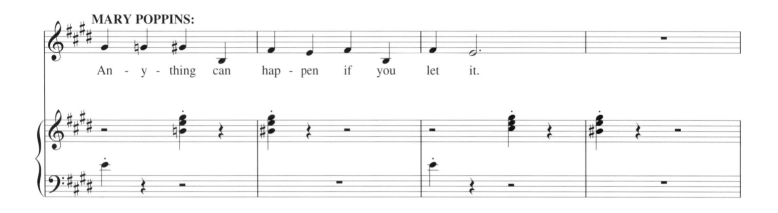

Mary Poppins is joined by chorus in this number, edited here as a solo.

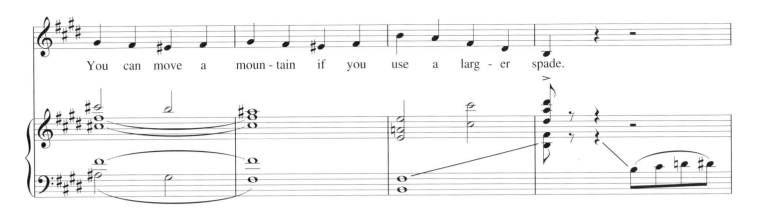

You can move a moun-tain if you use a larg-er spade.

An - y-thing can hap-pen, it's a mar-vel.

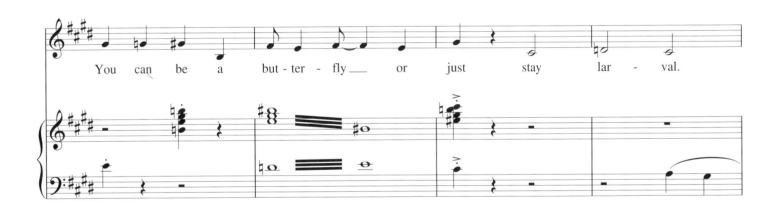

You can be a but-ter-fly___ or just stay lar-val.

Stretch your mind be - yond fan - tas - tic.

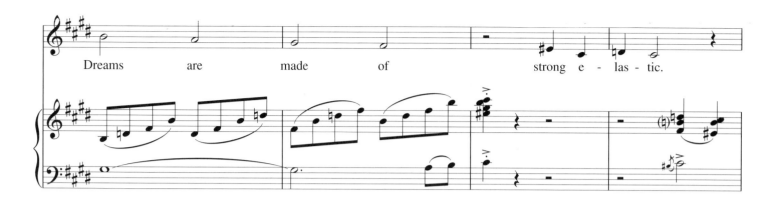

Dreams are made of strong e - las - tic.

Take some sound ad - vice and don't for - get it.

Più mosso ♩ = 106

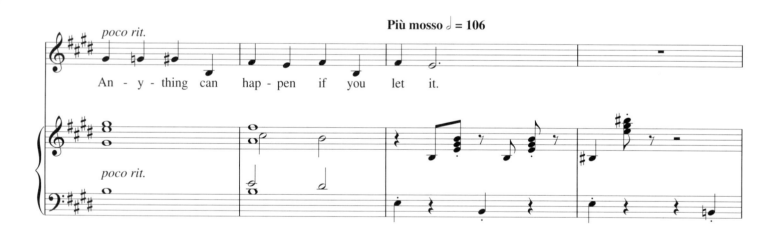

poco rit.

An - y - thing can hap - pen if you let it.

poco rit.

An - y - thing can hap - pen if you

let it. You won't know a chal-lenge un-til you've met it. No one does it for you, no one but your-self. Vac-il-lat-ing vi-o-lets get left up on the shelf. An-y-thing can hap-pen, raise the

cur - tain. Things you thought im - pos - si - ble will

soon seem cer - tain. Though at first it

may sound clown - ish, see the

world more up - side down - ish.

Turn it on its head then pir - ou - ette it.

An - y - thing can hap - pen if you let it.

Con moto ♩ = 120

If you reach for the stars, all you

get are the stars, but we've found a whole new

ONCE YOU LOSE YOUR HEART

from *Me And My Girl*

Words and Music by
NOEL GAY

Rubato, molto legato, cantabile

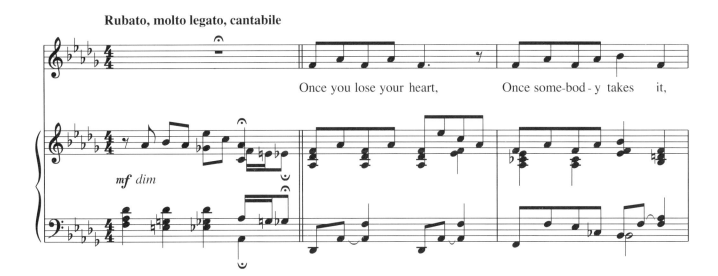

Once you lose your heart, Once some-bod-y takes it,

From the place it rest-ed in be-fore. Once you lose your heart,

Once some-bod-y wakes it, then it is-n't your heart an-y more. It's

SOMEBODY, SOMEWHERE

from *The Most Happy Fella*

By FRANK LOESSER

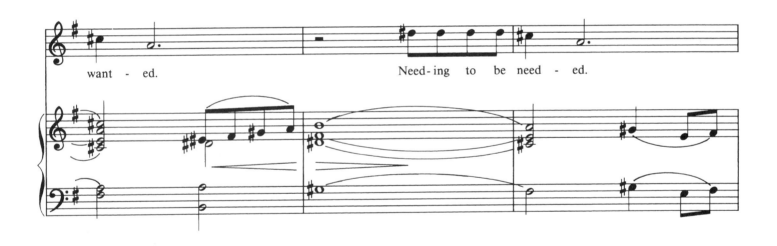

MY WHITE KNIGHT
from Meredith Willson's *The Music Man*

Words and Music by
MEREDITH WILLSON

Just some-one to love me, _ who is not a-shamed of a few nice things. My white knight; __ let me walk with him where the oth-ers ride by; Walk, and love him _ 'til I die. 'Til I die. __

MIGRATORY V
from *Myths And Hymns*

Music and Lyrics by
ADAM GUETTEL

Contemplative (♩. = 72)

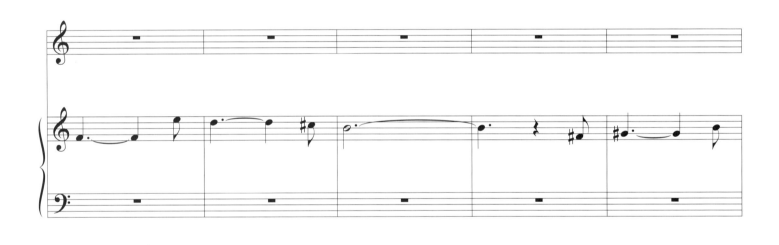

We

can_____ we fly_____ to - geth - er_____ a

mi - gra - tor - y V_____ How

won - der - ful_____ if____ that's_____ what God_____ could

see_____ A sin - gle voice in whis - pered prayer can on - ly

that's _____ what God could see. _____

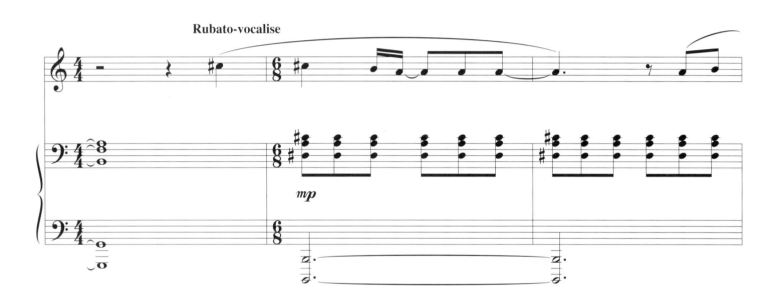

Rubato-vocalise

UNUSUAL WAY
(In a Very Unusual Way)
from *Nine*

Words and Music by
MAURY YESTON

Flowing (♪ = 84)

In a

ver-y un-u - su-al way, one time I need - ed you.
ver-y un-u - su-al way, I think I'm in love with you.

In a

ver-y un-u - su-al way, you were my friend.
ver-y un-u - su-al way, I want to cry.

how could I ev - er for-get __ you once __ you had touched __ my soul? __

In a ver - y un - u - su - al way, _____

you've made me _____

whole.

PEOPLE WILL SAY WE'RE IN LOVE
from *Oklahoma!*

Lyrics by OSCAR HAMMERSTEIN II
Music by RICHARD RODGERS

Laurey sings a verse, then Curley. This solo edition for soprano only presents Laurey's verse.

"don'ts" for you. Don't throw _____ bou-

quets at me _____ Don't please _____ my

folks too much _____ Don't laugh _____ at my

jokes too much _____ Peo - ple will say we're in

love! _____ Don't sigh _____ and gaze at me _____

Your sighs _____ are so like mine _____

Your eyes _____ must-n't glow like mine _____

Peo - ple will say we're in love! _____

Don't start ___ col - lect - ing things ___

Give me my rose and my glove. ___

Sweet - heart ___ they're sus - pect - ing things ___

Peo - ple will say we're in love. ___

MANY A NEW DAY

from *Oklahoma!*

Lyrics by OSCAR HAMMERSTEIN II
Music by RICHARD RODGERS

man I lose is the on-ly man a-mong men. I'll snap my fin-gers to

show I don't care, I'll buy me a brand new dress to wear, I'll scrub my neck and I'll

rit.

a tempo

brush my hair And start all o-ver a-gain.

a tempo, con ritmo

Refrain
Con grazia - non legato

Man-y a new face will please my eye, Man-y a new love will find me,

Nev-er-'ve I wan-dered through the rye, Won-der-in' where has some

guy gone, Man-y a new day will dawn be-fore I do!

Nev-er-'ve I chased the hon-ey bee who care-less-ly ca-

joled me, Some-bod-y else just as sweet as he, cheered me and con-

L.H.

ERRATA

A printing mistake occurred involving pages 114 and 115 of *Musical Theatre Essentials Soprano Volume 2*. The music which appears on page 115 should have been printed on page 114, and the music which appears on page 114 should have been printed on page 115. We apologize for the error and provide the correct order for these two pages in this insert.

Nev-er-'ve I once looked back to sigh o-ver the ro - mance be - hind me.

Man-y a new day will dawn be - fore I do! ____

Man-y a light lad may kiss and fly, A kiss gone by is by - gone,

Never-'ve I asked an Au - gust sky, "Where has last Ju - ly gone?"

Nev-er-'ve I once looked back to sigh o-ver the ro-mance be-hind me,

Man-y a new day will dawn be-fore I do!

Man-y a light lad may kiss and fly, A kiss gone by is by - gone,

Nev-er-'ve I asked an Au-gust sky, "Where has last Ju - ly gone?"

soled me. Nev-er-'ve I wept in - to my tea o- ver the deal some - one

doled me, Man-y a new day will dawn, Man-y a red sun will

poco rit.

set, Man- y a blue moon will shine, be - fore I

rit.

do!

f a tempo

I DON'T KNOW HIS NAME

from *She Loves Me*

Music by JERRY BOCK
Lyrics by SHELDON HARNICK

Moderato

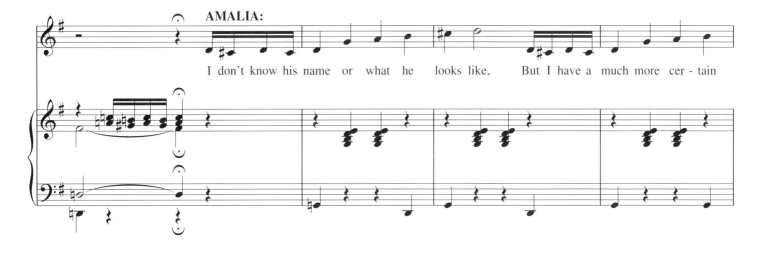

AMALIA:
I don't know his name or what he looks like, But I have a much more cer- tain

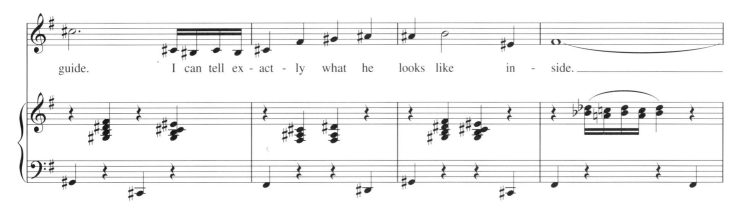

guide. I can tell ex- act- ly what he looks like in - side.

When I un- der- took this cor- res- pond- ence, lit- tle did I know I'd grow so

fond. Lit-tle did I know our views would so cor - res - pond. ___

___ He writes me what his feel - ings are on Shaw, Flau - bert, Cho-

pin, Ren - oir; The more I read the more I find we're one in mind and

heart. I know the kind of home we share, the books, the prints, the

music there. A home, a life that's warm and full and rich in love and

art. _____ I don't need to see his hand-some pro-file. I don't need to

see his man-ly frame. All I need to know is in each let-ter. Each long re-veal-ing

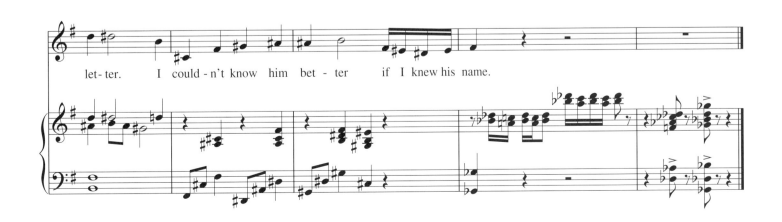

let-ter. I could-n't know him bet-ter if I knew his name.

WILL HE LIKE ME?

from *She Loves Me*

Words by SHELDON HARNICK
Music by JERRY BOCK

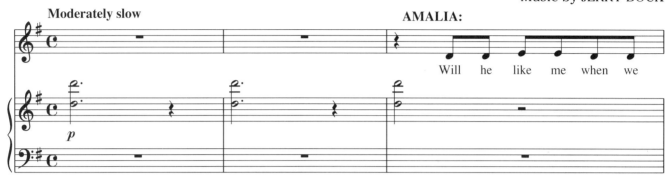

Moderately slow

AMALIA:

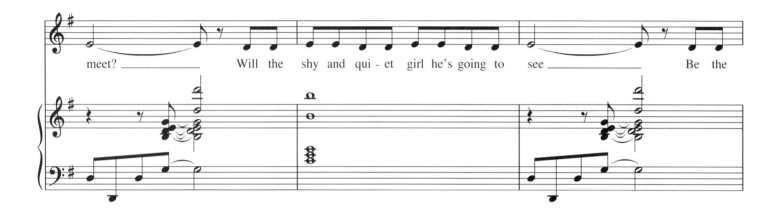

Will he like me when we meet? ____ Will the shy and qui-et girl he's going to see ____ Be the

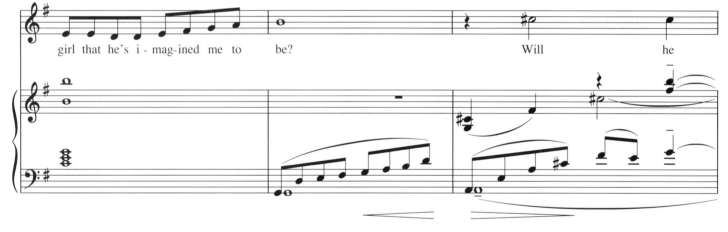

girl that he's i-mag-ined me to be? Will he like me?

like me? Will he like the girl he sees? ____ If he

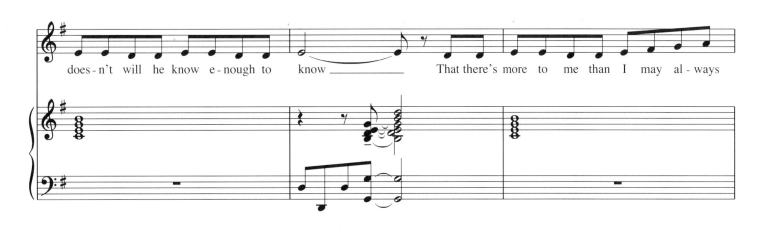

doesn't will he know enough to know _____ That there's more to me than I may always

show? Will he like me? Will he know that there's a

With more motion

world of love wait-ing to warm him? How I'm hop-ing that his

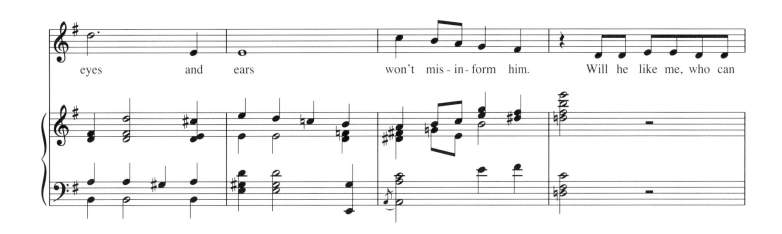

eyes and ears won't mis-in-form him. Will he like me, who can

Broaden

pen. _____ Will he know that there's a world of love

wait - ing to warm him? How I'm hop - ing that his eyes and

ears won't mis - in - form him. Will he like me? I don't

know. _____ All I know is that I'm tempt-ed not to go. _____ It's in -

san - i - ty for me to wor - ry so. I'll try

not to. Will he like me?

He's just got to. Will he like me?

Very slowly

Will he like me?

DEAR FRIEND

from *She Loves Me*

Words by SHELDON HARNICK
Music by JERRY BOCK

Poignantly (slowly)

AMALIA:

Charm - ing, ro - man - tic, the per - fect ca - fé.

Then as if it is - n't bad e - nough, a vi - o - lin starts to play.

Can - dles and wine, ta - bles for two,

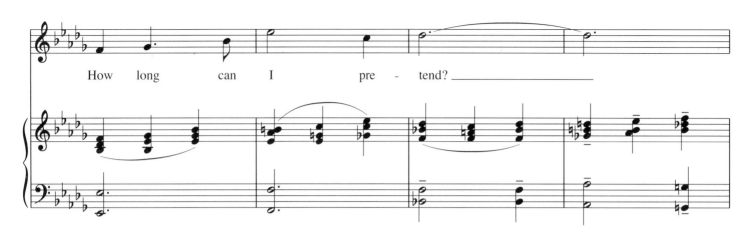

How long can I pre - tend?

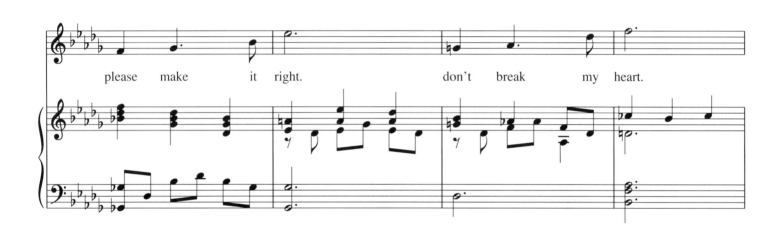

please make it right. don't break my heart.

Don't let it end, dear friend.

CAN'T HELP LOVIN' DAT MAN

from *Show Boat*

Lyrics by OSCAR HAMMERSTEIN II
Music by JEROME KERN

The original dialect in the lyric, printed here, may be adapted in performance to standard English.

man. _____ It mus' be sump-in' dat ___

___ de an - gels done plan. _____

p

Fish got to swim ___ and birds got to fly, ___ I got to love ___ one

man till I die. ___ Can't help lov-in' dat man ___ of mine. _____

* *This note presented as originally composed, has been changed in performance tradition to F rather than E-flat. The same is true for similar passages.*

The editor suggests the higher notes only on the repeat.

I HAVE CONFIDENCE

from *The Sound Of Music*

Music and Lyrics by
RICHARD RODGERS

Moderato (rubato)

What will this day be like? I won-der. _ What will my fu-ture

Più mosso

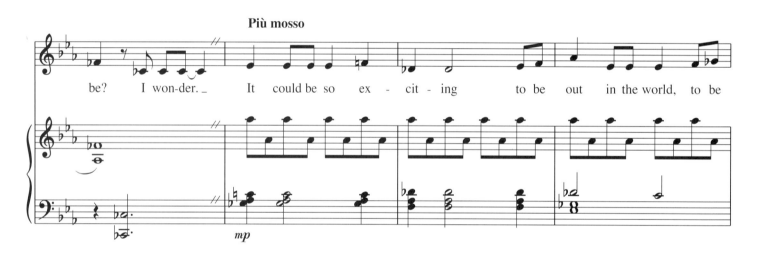

be? I won-der. _ It could be so ex-cit-ing to be out in the world, to be

free. My heart should be wild-ly re-joic-ing. Oh, what's the mat-ter with

Bright 2 *cresc. poco a poco*

me? I've al-ways longed for ad-ven - ture, _____ to do the

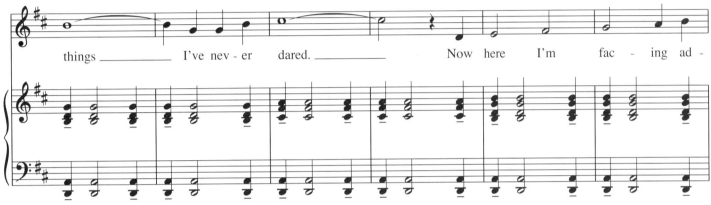

things _____ I've nev-er dared. _____ Now here I'm fac - ing ad-

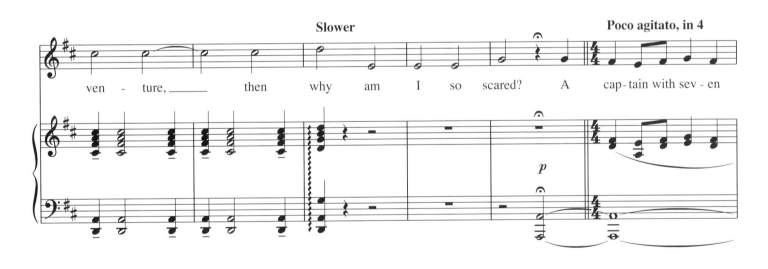

Slower **Poco agitato, in 4**

ven - ture, _____ then why am I so scared? A cap-tain with sev - en

Faster

chil-dren, what's so fear-some _ a-bout that? Oh, I must stop these doubts, all these wor - ries. If I

CLIMB EV'RY MOUNTAIN
from *The Sound Of Music*

Lyrics by OSCAR HAMMERSTEIN II
Music by RICHARD RODGERS

day of your life for as long as you live.

Poco pesante

Climb ev - 'ry moun - tain, Ford ev - 'ry stream.

Fol - low ev - 'ry rain - bow Till you find your

dream.

SOMETHING GOOD

from *The Sound Of Music*

Lyrics and Music by
RICHARD RODGERS

POPULAR
from the Broadway Musical *Wicked*

Music and Lyrics by
STEPHEN SCHWARTZ

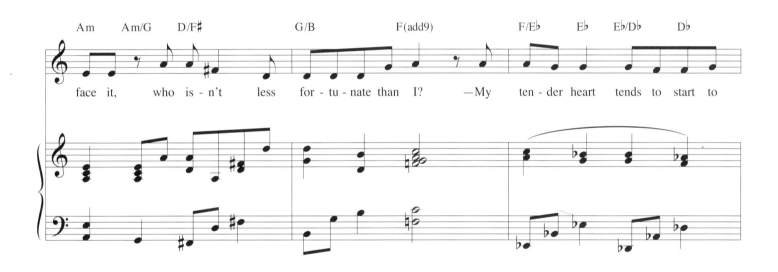

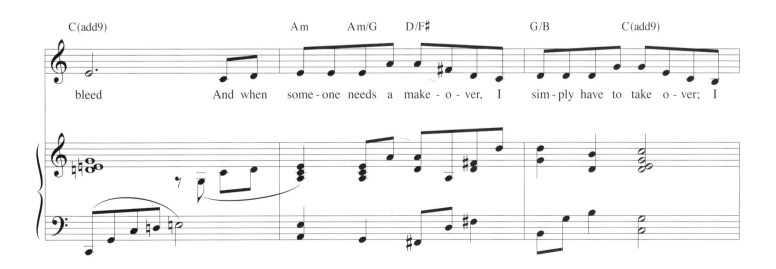

LET US BE GLAD
from the Broadway Musical *Wicked*

Music and Lyrics by
STEPHEN SCHWARTZ

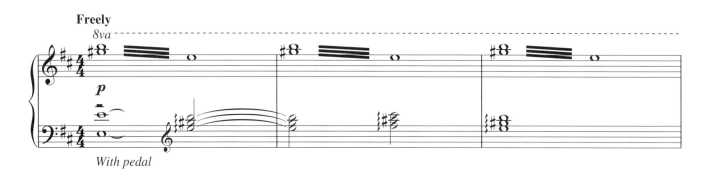

GLINDA:
Let us be glad, Let us be

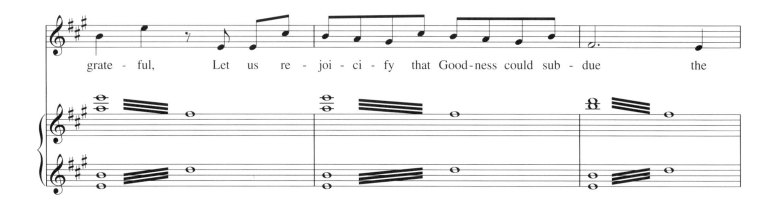

grate - ful, Let us re - joi - ci - fy that Good-ness could sub - due the

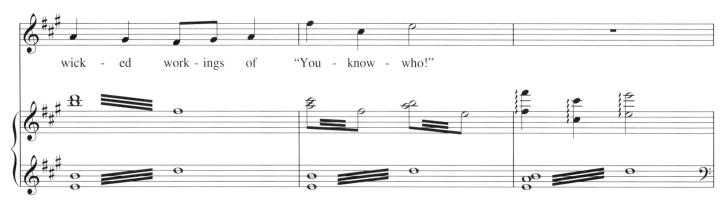

wick - ed work - ings of "You - know - who!"

Is - n't it nice to know   that good will con - quer

e - vil?   The truth we all be - lieve - 'll by and

Freely [*and softly*]

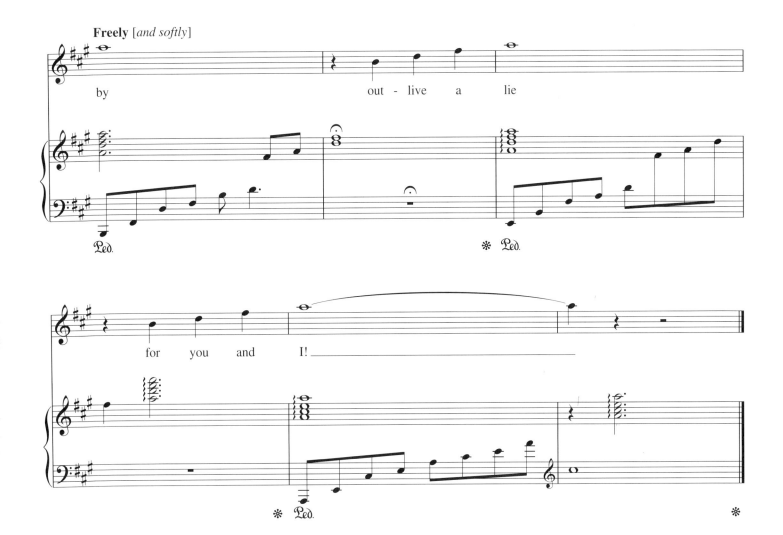

by   out - live a lie

for you and I!